Weather

David Keystone

Australia • Brazil • Japan • Korea • Mexico • Singapore • Spain • United Kingdom • United States

Weather

Text: David Keystone
Editor: Rebecca Crisp
Design: Kerri Wilson and Jess Kelly
Series design: James Lowe
Photo researcher: Libby Henry
Production controllers: Renee Cusmano and Lisa Porter
Reprint: Siew Han Ong

Acknowledgements
The author and publisher would like to acknowledge permission to reproduce material from the following sources:
Angelo Vlachoulis © Cengage Learning Australia: pp. 6, 8, 9 (top), 14–15 (main); Corbis Australia: pp. 1 (top inset), 4 (main), 17 (top right and bottom), 19 (both), 21 (main), 23 (top), cover (top inset); Fairfaxphotos/Rick Stevens: p. 18; Getty Images: pp. 1 (bottom inset), 4 (right inset), 7 (top), 9 (right), 10 (bottom), 13 (cumulonimbus), 16 (top), 17 (top left), 20, 21 (inset), cover (bottom inset), back cover; iStockphoto/Edyta Linek: pp. 1 (main), cover (main); Jupiterimages Corporation: pp. 5 (right), 10 (top); Newspix/ Alan Pryke: p. 22; Photolibrary: pp. 3, 4 (left inset), 5 (left), 7 (bottom), 9 (left), 11, 12 (both), 13 (cirrus), 13 (altostratus), 13 (stratus), 16 (bottom), 23 (bottom); Shutterstock/Daniela Sachsenheimer: p. 15 (inset); Shutterstock/Shebeko: p. 13 (cumulus).

Page 6: Illustration based on a map from the Bureau of Meterology, © Copyright Commonwealth of Australia 2008.

Fast Forward Independent Texts
Level 18

For product information and technology assistance,
in Australia call 1300 790 853;
in New Zealand call 0508 635 766

For permission to use material from this text or product,
please email **aust.permissions@cengage.com**

ISBN 978 0 17 017935 5
ISBN 978 0 17 017898 3 (set)

Cengage Learning Australia
Level 7, 80 Dorcas Street
South Melbourne, Victoria Australia 3205

Cengage Learning New Zealand
Unit 4B Rosedale Office Park
331 Rosedale Road, Albany, North Shore NZ 0632

For learning solutions, visit **cengage.com.au**

Printed in Australia by Ligare Pty Ltd
3 4 5 22 21 20

Weather

David Keystone

Contents

What Is Weather?

The weather is what is happening in the air outside right now.

It can be hot or cold,
wet or dry,
windy or still,
cloudy or clear.

The weather is not the same all over the world.
It may be warm and sunny in one place,
but cold and snowing in another.

Australia in January

the USA in January

The weather can change from day to day, and even from hour to hour.

The weather is affected by what is happening in the **atmosphere** each day.

Climate

Weather and **climate** are not the same thing.

Climate is the word used to talk about the weather in a place over a long time.

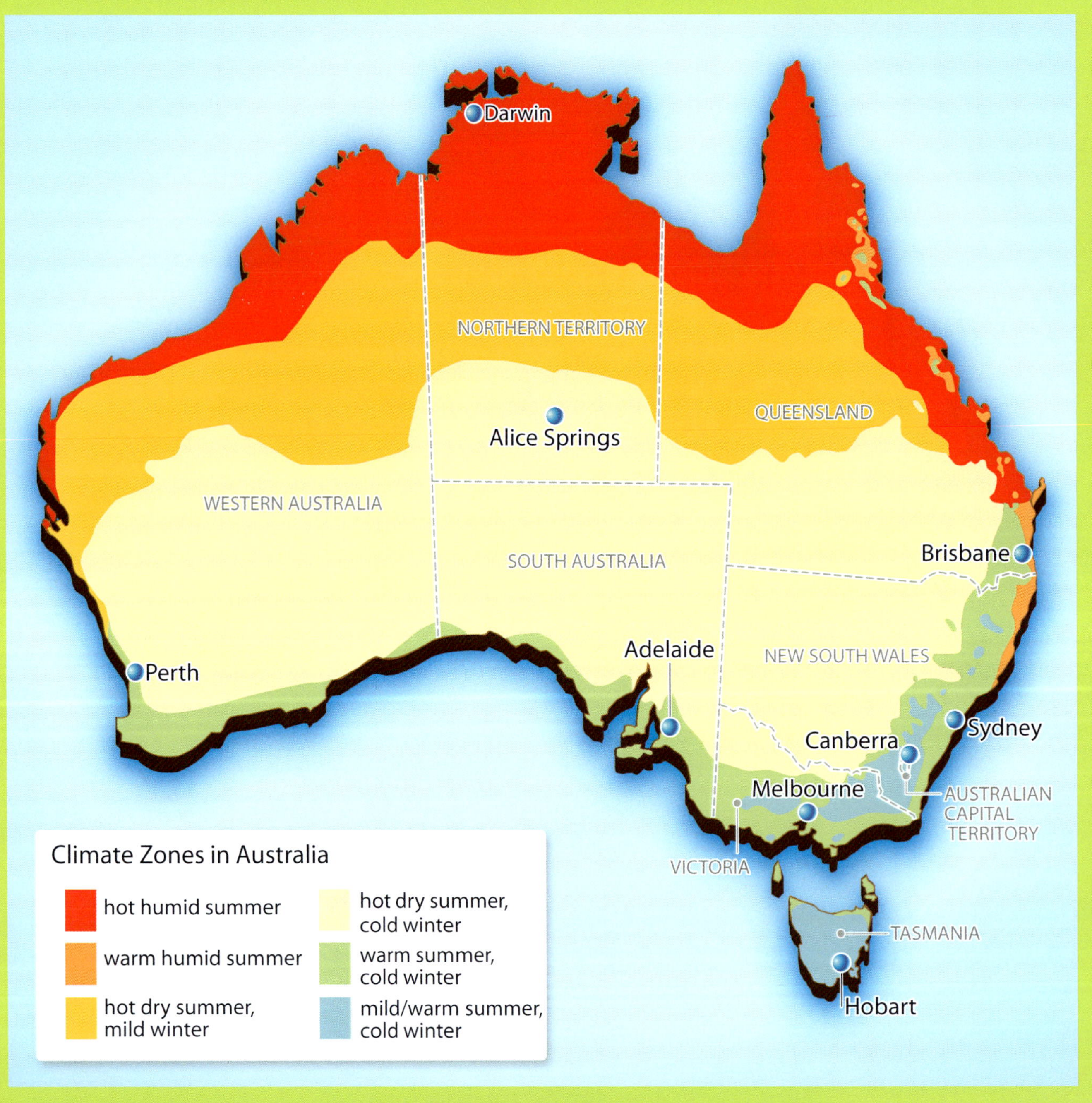

This map shows Australia's climate all year round.

While the weather can change
in just a few hours,
climate can take years to change.

In most places on Earth,
the climate is getting warmer.

In the mid-twentieth century, Mount Kilimanjaro had lots of snow on top.

Today, the snow has almost completely melted because of climate change.

Hot and Cold

The Sun controls the way the weather in one place changes throughout the year.

While Earth moves around the Sun,
it also spins around an **imaginary** line called an **axis**.
Earth's axis is **tilted**,
which means that different parts of Earth
are closer to the Sun at different times of the year.

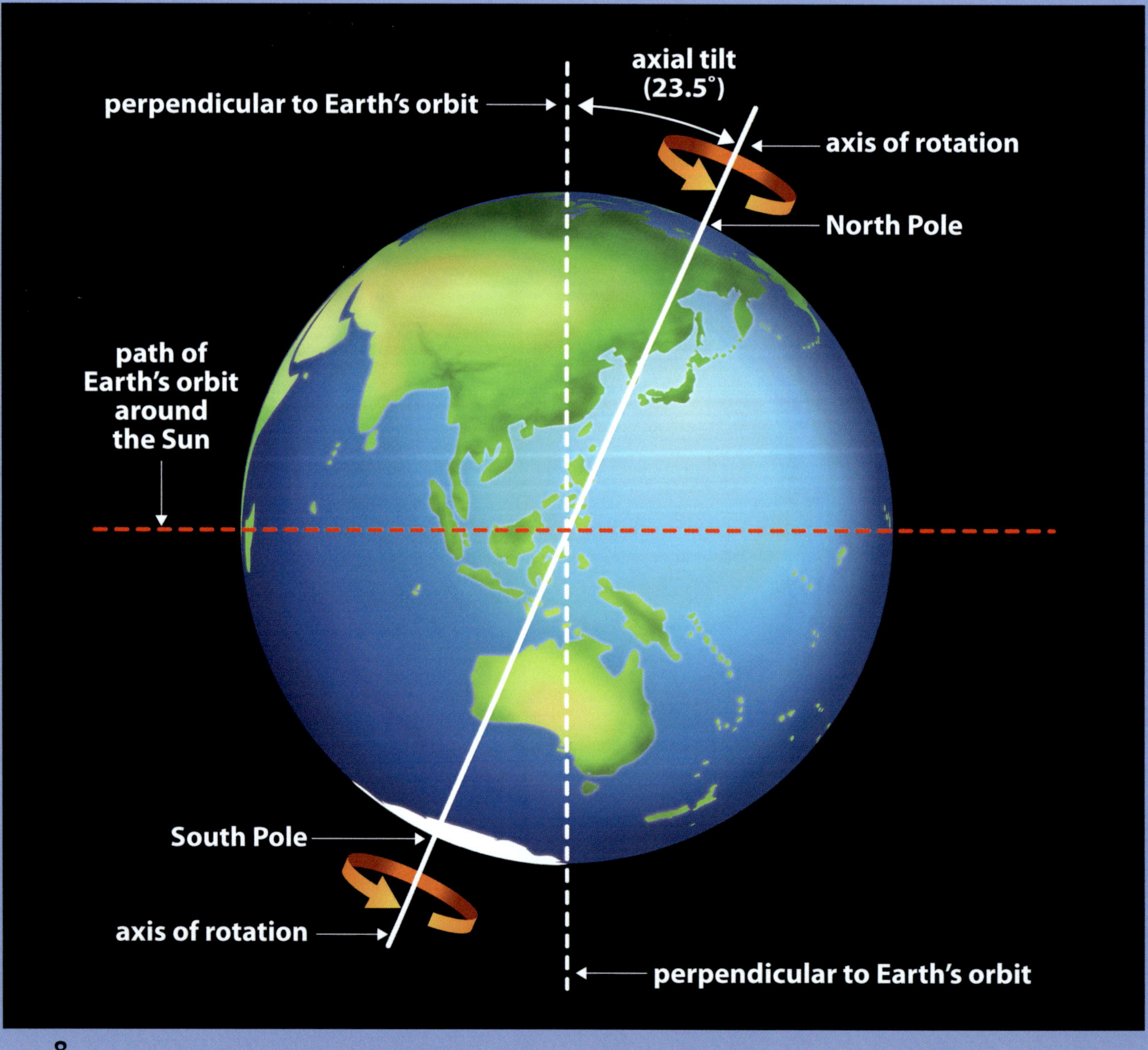

The side of Earth
that is tilted towards the Sun
gets more heat.
It is summer on that side of Earth.

The side that is tilted
away from the Sun is cooler.
It is winter on that side.

Japan in July (northern summer)

New Zealand in July (southern winter)

Earth's Orbit

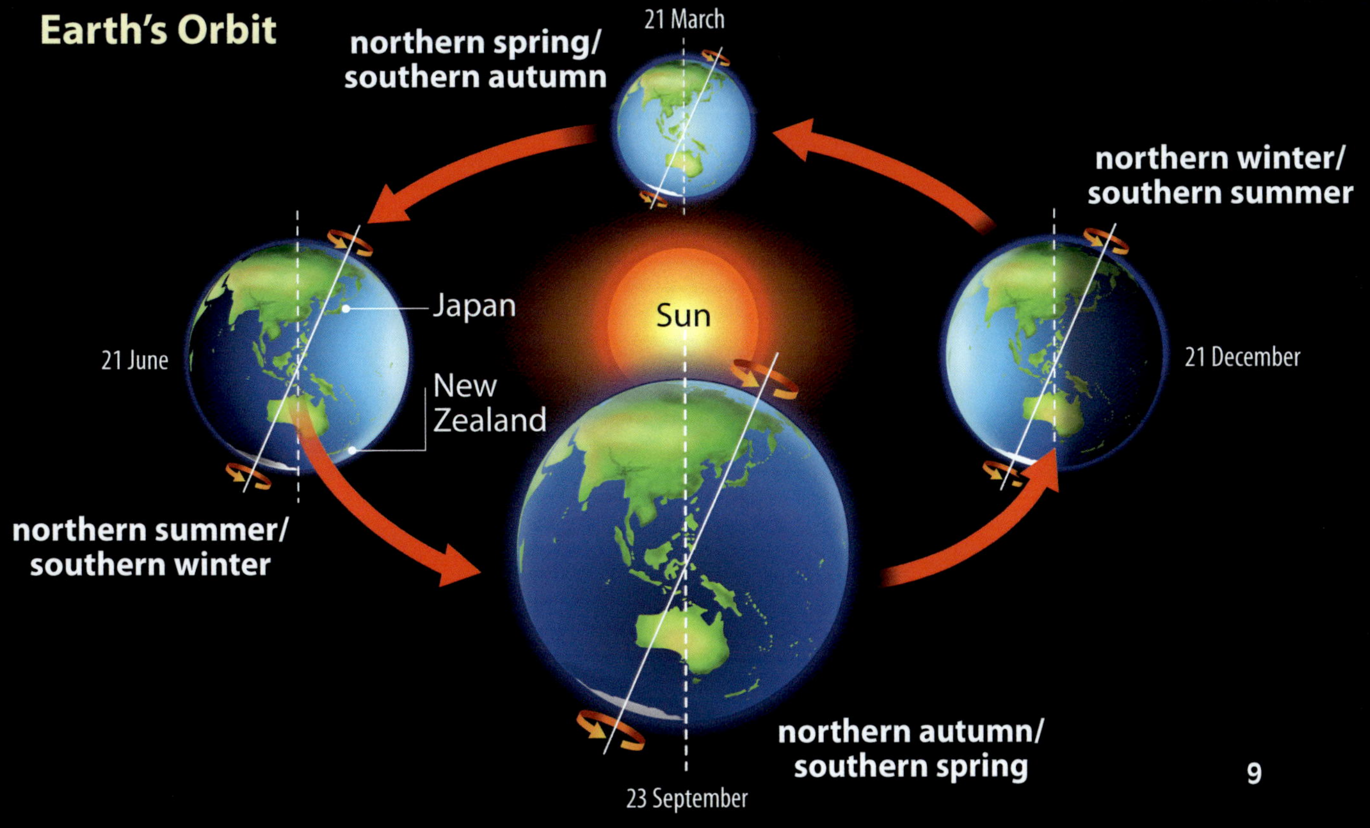

21 March

northern spring/ southern autumn

northern winter/ southern summer

21 June

Japan

New Zealand

Sun

21 December

northern summer/ southern winter

northern autumn/ southern spring

23 September

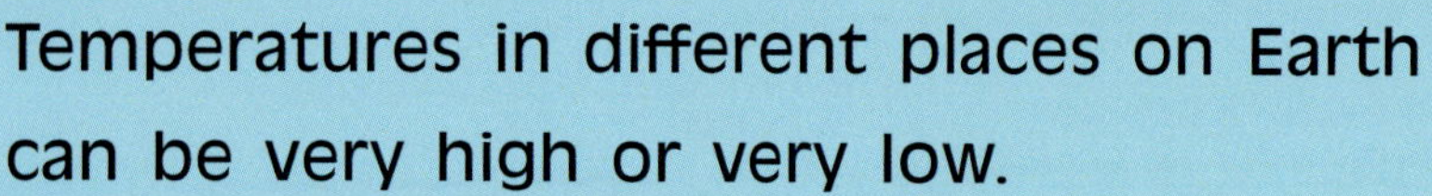

Temperatures in different places on Earth can be very high or very low.

The lowest temperature ever recorded was −89.2 °C in Antarctica.
The highest temperature ever recorded was 57.7 °C in Libya.

Antarctica

Libya

Types of Weather

Clouds and Rain

Clouds are made up
of many small drops of water **vapour**.
The drops are so light
that they can stay up in the air.
As the vapour gets cooler,
the drops become water
and they get heavier.

When the drops in the clouds become too heavy, they fall back to the ground as rain. Snow and hail form when the water in the clouds freezes before it falls as rain.

A rainbow appears when the Sun's light is bent by rain droplets and the white light splits into seven colours.

The rainbow colours always appear in the same order: red, orange, yellow, green, blue, indigo and violet.

Scientists can look at clouds to see if it is going to rain or snow.

Cloud Type	Height in Sky	Description	Type of Weather	What Cloud Looks Like
cirrus	high	thin white puffs	fair to sunny weather	
altostratus	mid	grey/blue-grey, covers the sky	rain or snow	
stratus	low	grey, even	very light rain	
cumulus	low	white, puffy, looks like cotton	fair weather	
cumulonimbus	low	large grey towers with flat tops	thunderstorms, heavy rain, snow, hail, lightning, tornadoes	

Wind

Wind is moving air.
The Sun makes the wind blow.
When the Sun heats Earth,
the air over the land gets warmer
than the air over the water.

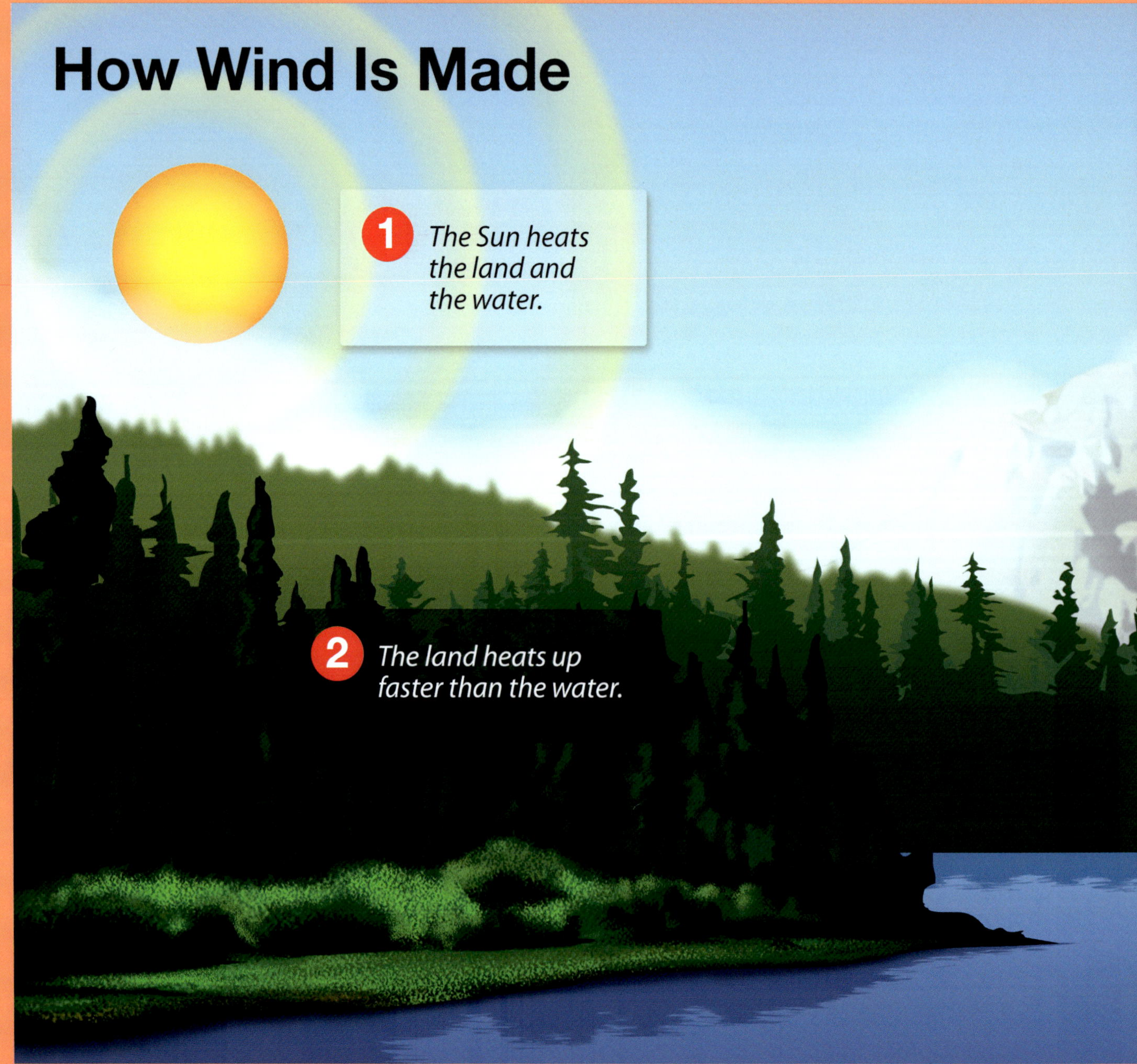

The warm air over the land rises
and the colder air over the water moves in to fill the gap.
This movement makes wind.

Scientists measure the speed of the wind and the way it is going.

a wind sock

CHAPTER 4

Extreme Weather

Sometimes the weather can be **extreme**. Extreme weather can be dangerous, and can have a big effect on people and the environment.

Too much rain can lead to floods, and not enough rain can lead to droughts.

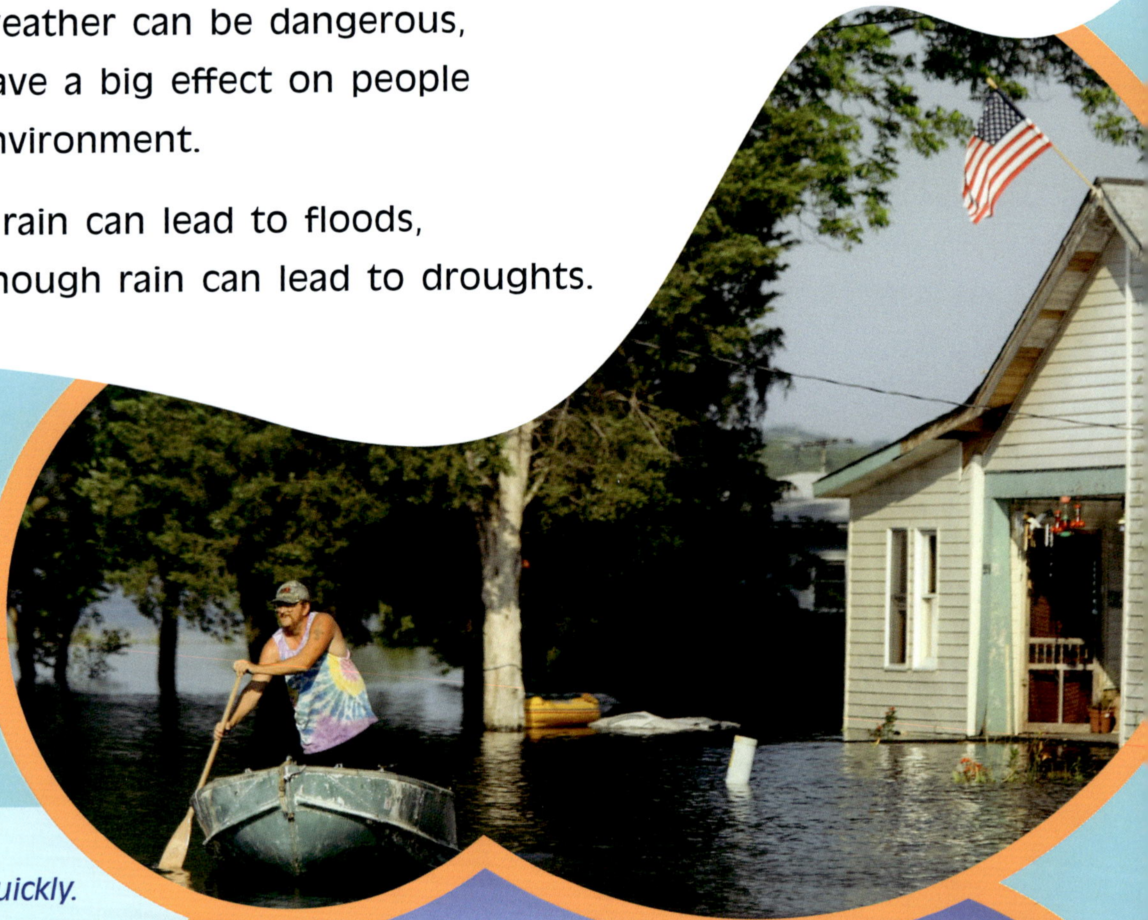

Floods can happen very quickly.

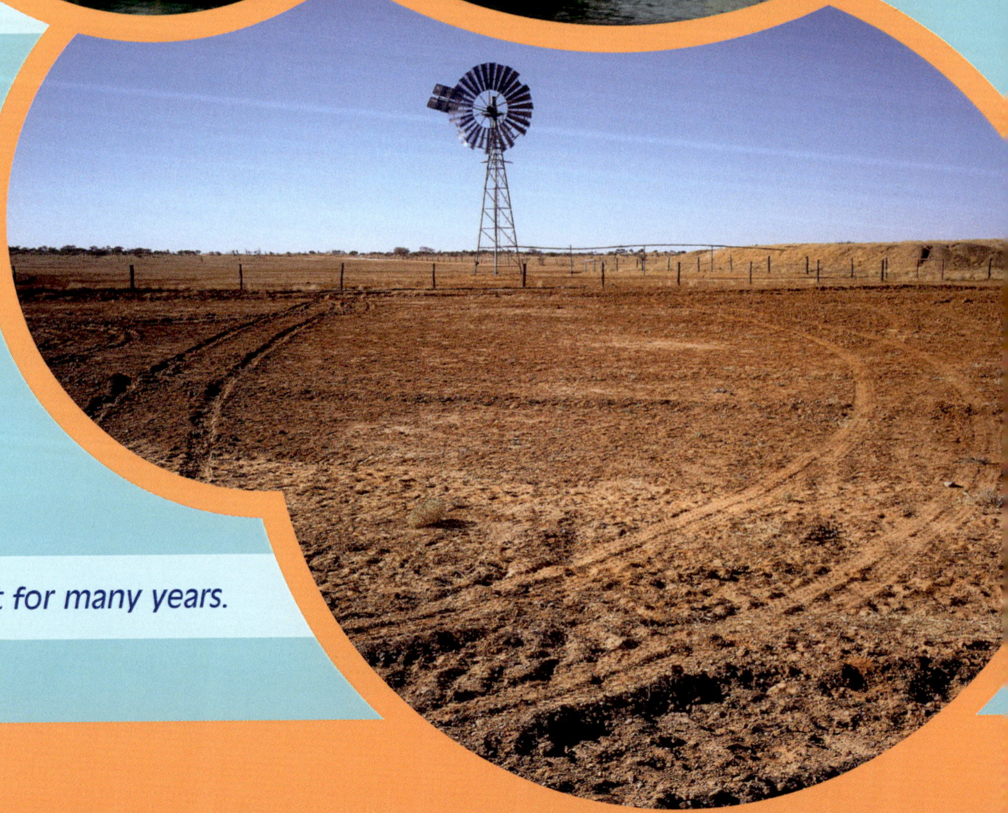

Droughts can last for many years.

Storms

In winter storms,
it can snow for many days.
People can get trapped
in buildings and cars.

A heavy snowstorm that lasts for more than a few days is called a blizzard.

Thunderstorms bring thunder and lightning.
Strong thunderstorms can also bring **flash-flooding** and strong winds.

If the thunder and lightning happen at the same time, the storm is very close.

Cyclones

Sometimes a thunderstorm can become huge,
and very strong.

In Australia,
these "super storms" are called **tropical cyclones**.

Cyclones develop over a warm sea.
They lose some of their strength
when they move over land.
Cyclones usually happen
in the warmer months.

On Christmas Eve, 1974, Cyclone Tracy hit Darwin, Australia.

In the USA,
"super storms" are called hurricanes.

In the western Pacific Ocean,
they are called typhoons.

a satellite photo of Hurricane Katrina

Hurricane Katrina killed at least 1836 people in the USA in 2005.

Heat Waves

Heat waves happen when the temperature in an area rises far above the usual temperature for three or more days.

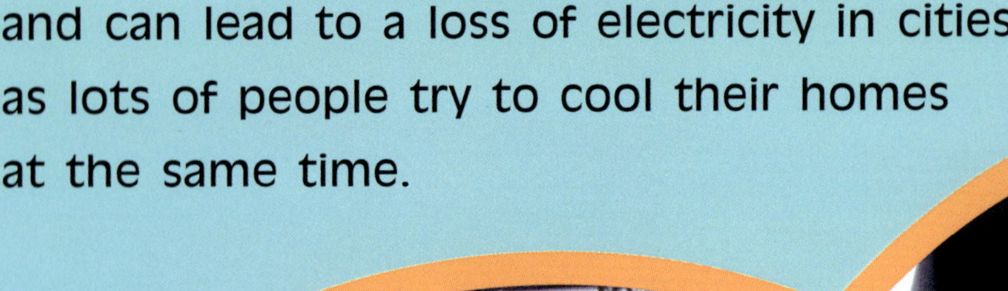

Heat waves can cause crops to die, and can lead to a loss of electricity in cities as lots of people try to cool their homes at the same time.

When lots of people in a city turn their air-conditioners on, it can overload the city's electricity supply, and lead to a blackout.

In 2003, a heat wave hit Western Europe.
About 35 000 people died
because they could not keep cool enough.
Some people died in bushfires
that started due to the very dry conditions.

It is important to drink lots of water in a heat wave
and to stay in a cool place.

a bushfire burning in Spain during the 2003 European heat wave

Knowing the Weather

It is important to know about the weather because it affects people every day.

Weather affects what people choose to wear and what they choose to do.

Knowing about the weather helps people to stay safe.
When people know about the weather,
they can be ready for anything.

Glossary

atmosphere — the air that surrounds Earth

axis — the imaginary line around which Earth spins

climate — the most common weather conditions seen in a place over a number of years

extreme — farthest from the ordinary or average

flash-flooding — flooding that happens very quickly

imaginary — not real or actual

tilted — leaning on an angle

tropical cyclones — very strong storms with high winds and heavy rain. Also called hurricanes, tornadoes and typhoons

vapour — water in the form of gas

Index